MAX RIDE
FIRST FLIGHT

JAMES PATTERSON

COLLECTION EDITOR *MARK D. BEAZLEY*
ASSISTANT EDITOR *SARAH BRUNSTAD*
ASSOCIATE MANAGING EDITOR *ALEX STARBUCK*
EDITOR, SPECIAL PROJECTS *JENNIFER GRÜNWALD*
SENIOR EDITOR, SPECIAL PROJECTS *JEFF YOUNGQUIST*
SVP PRINT, SALES & MARKETING *DAVID GABRIEL*
BOOK DESIGNER *ADAM DEL RE*

EDITOR IN CHIEF *AXEL ALONSO*
CHIEF CREATIVE OFFICER *JOE QUESADA*
PUBLISHER *DAN BUCKLEY*
EXECUTIVE PRODUCER *ALAN FINE*

MAX RIDE: FIRST FLIGHT. CONTAINS MATERIAL ORIGINALLY PUBLISHED IN MAGAZINE FORM AS MAX RIDE: FIRST FLIGHT #1-5. FIRST PRINTING 2015. ISBN# 978-0-7851-9742-3. PUBLISHED BY MARVEL WORLDWIDE, INC., A SUBSIDIARY OF MARVEL ENTERTAINMENT, LLC. OFFICE OF PUBLICATION: 135 WEST 50TH STREET, NEW YORK, NY 10020. COPYRIGHT © 2015 BY JAMES PATTERSON. ALL RIGHTS RESERVED. ALL CHARACTERS FEATURED IN THIS ISSUE AND THE DISTINCTIVE NAMES AND LIKENESSES THEREOF, AND ALL RELATED INDICIA ARE TRADEMARKS OF JAMES PATTERSON. NO SIMILARITY BETWEEN ANY OF THE NAMES, CHARACTERS, PERSONS, AND/OR INSTITUTIONS IN THIS MAGAZINE WITH THOSE OF ANY LIVING OR DEAD PERSON OR INSTITUTION IS INTENDED, AND ANY SUCH SIMILARITY WHICH MAY EXIST IS PURELY COINCIDENTAL. MARVEL AND ITS LOGOS ARE TM MARVEL CHARACTERS, INC. **PRINTED IN THE U.S.A.** ALAN FINE, PRESIDENT, MARVEL ENTERTAINMENT; DAN BUCKLEY, PRESIDENT, TV, PUBLISHING AND BRAND MANAGEMENT; JOE QUESADA, CHIEF CREATIVE OFFICER; TOM BREVOORT, SVP OF PUBLISHING; DAVID BOGART, SVP OF OPERATIONS & PROCUREMENT, PUBLISHING; C.B. CEBULSKI, VP OF INTERNATIONAL DEVELOPMENT & BRAND MANAGEMENT; DAVID GABRIEL, SVP PRINT, SALES & MARKETING; JIM O'KEEFE, VP OF OPERATIONS & LOGISTICS; DAN CARR, EXECUTIVE DIRECTOR OF PUBLISHING TECHNOLOGY; SUSAN CRESPI, EDITORIAL OPERATIONS MANAGER; ALEX MORALES, PUBLISHING OPERATIONS MANAGER; STAN LEE, CHAIRMAN EMERITUS. FOR INFORMATION REGARDING ADVERTISING IN MARVEL COMICS OR ON MARVEL.COM, PLEASE CONTACT JONATHAN RHEINGOLD, VP OF CUSTOM SOLUTIONS & AD SALES, AT JRHEINGOLD@MARVEL.COM. FOR MARVEL SUBSCRIPTION INQUIRIES, PLEASE CALL 800-217-9158. **MANUFACTURED BETWEEN 7/31/2015 AND 9/7/2015 BY R.R. DONNELLEY, INC., SALEM, VA, USA.**

10 9 8 7 6 5 4 3 2 1

ADAPTED FROM THE NOVEL,
MAXIMUM RIDE
BY **JAMES PATTERSON**

WRITER
MARGUERITE BENNETT

PENCILER
ALEX SANCHEZ

INKERS
ALEX SANCHEZ (#1-3) & **MARK PENNINGTON** (#3-5)

COLORIST
ESTHER SANZ

LETTERER
VC'S TRAVIS LANHAM

COVER ARTISTS
STEPHANIE HANS & **YASMINE PUTRI** (#2)

ASSISTANT EDITOR
CHARLES BEACHAM

EDITOR
SANA AMANAT

Congratulations on slipping the surly bonds of Earth! You're airborne. You're airborne with a story that has perhaps the most dedicated following of any I've written (my publisher tells me it's had more than 20 million readers, and counting). You're airborne with the wizards of Marvel, those guys who have created the most successful pantheon of heroes in the modern era. You're airborne with Maximum Ride and the greatest development in all of human evolution: your brain.

Of course, you've been up here before. Those of us who read books (illustrated and not) know a little secret, don't we? That reading a story can be a more intense and pleasurable experience than any film, game, or amusement-park ride.

It's not always the case. Some graphic novels (and many, many regular novels) don't manage to get our minds and spirits aloft. But when they work—when they're good—go ahead and grab your knees and say goodbye to terra firma.

You're a reader. You know what I'm talking about.

Anyhow, I happen to know that the Maximum Ride novels achieved this effect on many people. Tens of millions of them. No other story has generated more fan mail for me, nor generated more spontaneous online content. There are tens if not hundreds of thousands of fan videos, drawings, and fan fictions out there featuring Maximum Ride.

So when Marvel came to me and said they wanted to take a crack at doing their own rendition of Max, I was all ears. The people who brought Spider-Man, the Avengers, the X-Men, and so many more iconic cultural figures into living color have here taken their own brilliant talents to my Max, and I think she's only the better for it.

I think you'll find even if you've read the books already that this adaptation is more than an adaptation. This is a whole new flight. My only instructions to them were to make it fly, and they've done that.

I'm not going to get all gooey on you here and say Marvel's the wind beneath my wings or anything, but the writers and artists and editors did do something rare here: they took a fresh vision of an existing story and they got it (and all its characters) aloft.

Which probably is all part of some gigantic cosmic metaphor here. I mean, a big part of the reason I dreamed up Max in the first place was that I have always been fascinated by flight. That idea of being able to just take off into the air and look down on the world, to get from point A to point B (or discover undreamt-of point C) like a bird, or like a dream, or like when you're experiencing a great story—it's a pretty cool experience.

So please don't let me hold you back here. Turn the page and go take flight with a bunch of mutant kids who will change how you see the world.

Please, enjoy the elevation, and the Ride.

All my best,

JP

CHAPTER 1

...FOR THE *FAMILY* HE GAVE ME.

FANG, NUDGE, IGGY, GAZZY AND ANGEL-- ORPHANS LIKE ME, *EXPERIMENTS* LIKE ME.

JEB ADOPTED US. WE ADOPTED EACH OTHER.

MORNING, NUDGE! WHAT'RE WE HAVING?

THE CHEF HAS SELECTED AN ARRAY OF *RICOTTA* CREPES WITH THE BLUEBERRY COMPOTE, WITH A COMPLEMENT OF *FRESH* CINNAMON CIABATTA ROLLS AND LOCAL SEASONAL FRUIT.

REALLY?

NOPE. *PANCAKES* AGAIN.

NICE OF YOU TO JOIN US, NOW THAT THE WORK IS DONE.

HA! *FANG,* YOU DON'T WANT ME AT THAT STOVE.

I SURVIVED FOURTEEN YEARS OF HELL AT THAT SCHOOL. NONE OF WHICH PREPARED ME FOR YOUR COOKING.

YOU DOING DISHES OR AM I A SINGLE PARENT OVER HERE?

MORNING, IGGY, GASMAN. WHOSE LAPTOP DIED FOR TODAY'S EXPERIMENTS, GAZZY?

THE INTERNET IS OUR LINK TO THE OUTSIDE WORLD, MAX. IT'S OUR MOST *IMPORTANT* RESOURCE!

IT'S FANG'S. DON'T TELL HIM.

HEY!

I COUNT FIVE OF US...WE ARE MISSING ONE BOTTOMLESS PIT. WHERE'S ANGEL...?

I'LL GET HER!

I CAN SEE THE TOMBSTONE NOW.

"HE DIED AS HE LIVED--THE HANDSOMEST MAN AT THE WEREWOLF RODEO."

GENETICALLY MODIFIED STRENGTH AND SPEED--

BUT THEY STILL COULDN'T ENGINEER YOU A WAY TO *SHUT UP.*

MAAAAX!

NO!

ANGEL!!

HOW FAR ARE WE, IGGY?

WE'VE ALL GOT OUR SKILLS, COURTESY OF THE GENE SPLICING. I'D GET LOST IN THE CORNER OF A ROUND ROOM, BUT IGGY'S A HUMAN COMPASS.

WE'RE DEFINITELY IN CALIFORNIA. I'M GUESSING NOT FAR FROM LAKE TAHOE.

WE'RE GOING TO NEED TO EAT SOON. OUR METABOLISMS ARE TOO HIGH TO SUSTAIN THIS MUCH ACTIVITY WITHOUT THE NUTRIENTS TO MATCH.

I'LL GO FOR SUPPLIES.

BE CAREFUL, MAX.

I'M PRETTY SURE I'M THE APEX PREDATOR AROUND HERE.

UMM, DID YOU SEE WHAT FLEW INTO OUR HOUSE?

RUDE.

HURRY BACK, MAX. WE'LL BE WAITING.

CHAPTER 2

THE SMELL OF GUN SMOKE CUTS THROUGH THE AIR AS THE SPENT CASING FALLS TO THE GROUND.

I CAN FEEL THE RUSH OF ADRENALINE IN MY VEINS, MAKING ME DIZZY, FEATHER-LIGHT.

THE TASTE OF MY BLOOD FILLS MY MOUTH, STINGING *HOT* AND *TANG* LIKE COPPER.

I CAN HEAR THE DRUMBEAT OF THEIR SHOES ON THE PAVEMENT FARTHER AND FAINTER AND AWAY...

BUT ALL I SEE...

STOP SAYING THAT!

IT IS **NOT** GOING TO BE OKAY! NOT UNLESS WE DO SOMETHING!

WHAT CAN WE DO?! THEY TOOK ANGEL, DESTROYED OUR HOUSE! MAX ISN'T EVEN HERE.

SHE MIGHT BE WOUNDED-- SHE MIGHT BE **DEAD!**

DON'T SAY THAT! MAX IS **FINE.**

THE ERASERS AREN'T HERE YET SO WE'VE GOT TIME. WE NEED TO STAY PUT SO MAX CAN FIND US.

WELL IF WE'RE STAYING HERE WE NEED A PLAN.

WE NEED TO HIDE, BUT WE HAVE TO BE CLOSE ENOUGH TO SIGNAL MAX ON SIGHT.

US OR THE ERASERS. **ONE'S GOTTA MAKE LIKE A BIRD AND FLOCK OFF.**

FANG, I SWEAR. I NEVER THOUGHT ONE OF YOUR STUPID PUNS WOULD ACTUALLY BE **HELPFUL--**

...IGGY?

I'VE GOT A PLAN.

TRACKER!
E ERASERS
ROBABLY
OW RIGHT
ERE I AM.
I'VE PUT
LA AND DR.
MARTINEZ
N DANGER.

I WAS AN *IDIOT* TO COME HERE, I WAS AN IDIOT TO LET DOWN MY GUARD... TO EVEN PRETEND--

I'VE GOT TO GET TO ANGEL--

I NEED TO GO.

WAIT!

TAKE SOME FOOD AND MEDICAL SUPPLIES FOR YOUR JOURNEY.

AND HERE'S OUR NUMBER, IF YOU NEED HELP.

PEOPLE.

PEOPLE ARE DANGEROUS.

REGULAR, ORDINARY, EVERYDAY PEOPLE.

NOT BECAUSE THEY TRY TO HURT YOU...

SAY GOODBYE TO ELLA FOR ME.

OF COURSE.

BE SAFE, SWEETHEART.

BUT BECAUSE YOU *MISS* THEM WHEN THEY'RE GONE.

THEY MAKE YOU WANT TO FOLD YOUR WINGS...

CHAPTER 3

CRNCH

YOU'RE A LIAR, ARI.

YOU'RE GONNA MAKE ME A ROAST FREAKING CHICKEN BECAUSE YOU'RE A--

ACH!

FWOOOM

MAX!

SHE'S OUT COLD AND **SHAKING**-- WE NEED TO GET HER SOMEWHERE **SAFE**--

YOU KNOW, IN MOVIES GUYS ARE ALWAYS LIKE, "SHE BARELY WEIGHED ANYTHING AT ALL," BUT YOU KNOW WHAT?

GIRLS ARE **HEAVY**.

IS SHE OKAY? THE MONEY WE MADE ON THE SUBWAY DIDN'T GO FAR, MAYBE SHE DIDN'T EAT ENOUGH--

I DON'T KNOW. SHE'S BEEN SO SECRETIVE SINCE THE SCHOOL...

WE NEED TO FIND A PLACE TO LAY LOW. EVEN SINGING OR BEGGING ON THE CORNER, WE COULDN'T GET A HOSTEL FOR ALL OF US.

AND A HOMELESS SHELTER...IF THE ERASERS CAME, THAT WOULD BE THE FIRST PLACE THEY'D CHECK.

WE NEED...

HERE. DOWN HERE.

WHAT?

DOWN HERE. I'M NOT KIDDING. I HAVE NO IDEA WHAT THIS MEANS, BUT **EVERY INSTINCT** IS TELLING ME **HERE**, DOWN HERE IS **SAFE**.

IT'S LIKE A COMPASS IN THE PIT OF MY STOMACH.

IT'S LIKE SOME SIDE EFFECT, SOME POWER I DIDN'T EVEN KNOW WAS MINE...

...BUT IT KNOWS...THIS IS THE PLACE WE NEED TO BE.

HANG IN THERE.

WE'LL TAKE CARE OF YOU, MAX. I PROMISE.

WE NEED YOU.

CHAPTER 3

CHAPTER 4

SERIOUSLY! WHAT DID YOU DO TO MY COMPUTERS?!

THIS ISN'T-- THIS WAS IN MY DREAM, IT CAN'T-- I DIDN'T DO THIS!!

MAXIMUM, IT'S OKAY, IT--

AH!

AH!

NO! ANGEL, I'M SO SORRY...!

SHH! IT'S OKAY, MAX.

I HEARD IT TOO. WHEN I TOUCHED YOU, I HEARD IT TOO.

AND I THINK... I KNOW WHAT TO DO.

WHAM

YOU KNOW, ARI, YOU MUTT-- FANG HAD THIS JOKE HE WAS DYING TO USE LAST TIME--

LET'S BLOW THIS PUPSICLE STAND.

(GET IT? HE'S A DOG.)

FANG!

...THIS IS PERFECT.

IT'S A...BAY HOUSE!

A WHAT?

THESE OLD FISHING COTTAGES IN THE MARSHES. THEY'RE ABANDONED BUT PEOPLE ARE TOO SCARED THAT DESTROYING THEM WILL HARM THE LOCAL ECOSYSTEM--

NUDGE, WHAT IS GOING ON WITH YOU? HOW DO YOU KNOW ALL THIS STUFF?

I DON'T KNOW! IT'S LIKE EVERY PLACE WE COME TO, I GET THIS FLASH OF WHAT IT USED TO BE-- LIKE I CAN FEEL ITS HISTORY, ITS PURPOSE--

THE BOTTOM LINE IS, IT SOUNDS LIKE WE'RE SAFE HERE. NO ONE'S GOING TO COME SNOOPING AROUND A PLACE THIS DILAPIDATED.

MAX, THIS BLANKET SMELLS LIKE FISH.

SHH.

WE'VE BEEN RUNNING, GUNNING, OVERWHELMED...AND EVERY CLUE WE FIND ABOUT WHERE WE CAME FROM SEEMS TO BE BOOBY-TRAPPED.

WE'VE GOT TO REST...

-YAWN-

BREAKFAST, YOU RABBLE!

ANYONE EVER TELL YOU THAT YOU SNORE LIKE AN OGRE? THEY DEFINITELY SPLICED SOME BEAR OR RHINO INTO YOUR DNA, I MEAN, JEEZ, WOMAN--

YOU BROUGHT ME THE TABLOIDS?

PAGE 6. "MUTANT BIRD CHILDREN OF NEW YORK." OUR ESCAPE FROM THE INSTITUTE OF HIGHER LEARNING COULD'VE BEEN MORE... FINESSED.

SPEAKING OF MUTANTS...

YOU FINDING IT A LITTLE WEIRD THAT WE ALL SEEM TO BE DEVELOPING THESE...ABILITIES?

DECISIVELY AND PARTICULARLY ATTUNED TO HELPING US SURVIVE THIS KAFKAESQUE NIGHTMARE OF TECHNOHORROR AND JACK-IN-THE-BOX WEREWOLVES?

IGGY'S A HUMAN COMPASS. NUDGE CAN COMMUNE WITH OBJECTS. ANGEL CAN READ MINDS.

WHAT CAN I DO?

YOU CAN BLOW STUFF UP, GASMAN. THAT'S PRETTY SICK.

OH YEAH.

MADAME, I AM WOUNDED.

BUT YOU'LL LIVE.

NO. I DIDN'T STEAL. SOME PEOPLE PAY MONEY FOR MY HUMOR!

MASOCHISTS.

WHICH, Y'KNOW, I GUESS WE HAVE TO BE BY THIS POINT. IF WE WEREN'T SUCH SUCKERS FOR PUNISHMENT, WE'D GIVE UP THIS MISSION.

WHAT IF... WE DID JUST FORGET ALL THAT FOR THE TIME BEING?

FANG--?

LOOK AT ANGEL. SHE'S HAPPY.

THEY'RE ALL HAPPY.

WHEN IS THE LAST TIME YOU COULD SAY THAT OF US? OF ANY OF US?

I JUST NEED--

I JUST NEED YOU.

DON'T SCREAM, MAX. YOU DON'T WANT TO WAKE THE OTHERS.

SLEEP IS VERY IMPORTANT FOR YOUR DEVELOPMENT.

AM I... DREAMING?

ERASERS...

THOUSANDS OF THEM.

THAT'S WHY SHE NAMED YOU MAXIMUM.

WHO?

YOUR MOTHER.

CHAPTER 5

IN THE SEWERS BENEATH NEW YORK CITY.

DEATH VALLEY. THE BOGS OF LONG ISLAND. THE NEW YORK CITY SEWER SYSTEM.

I'M JUST SAYING, WE NEVER GET TO GO ON A RECONNAISSANCE MISSION TO THE *SOUTH OF FRANCE*, YOU KNOW? NO REVENGE QUESTS TO HAWAII--

FANG, SHUT IT, OR I *WILL* FEED YOU TO A CROCODILE.

THOSE ARE A MYTH, RIGHT, IGGY?

SO ARE THE WINGED BIRD CHILDREN OF MANHATTAN.

TOUCHÉ.

I CAN FEEL... PEOPLE, WHO WERE HERE BEFORE US.

WE'RE GETTING CLOSE, GUYS...THE PLACE WE NEED IS UP AHEAD.

I CAN HEAR... VOICES. MINDS, I MEAN.

WHAT ARE THEY SAYING, ANGEL?

NOTHING... THEY'RE JUST SO SAD.

THEY'RE RUNNING SO MUCH POWER THROUGH HERE-- THIS MUST BE THE REAL DEAL. NOT LIKE THAT RECORDS ROOM.

IN THE BOTTOM OF THE SEWER...

...THE INSTITUTE OF HIGHER LEARNING.

THAT'S A FANCY LOCK...

HOW ARE WE GONNA GET INSIDE?

DON'T LOOK AT ME. I NAVIGATED US HERE. MY PART IN OPERATION CERTAIN DOOM IS DONE...GAZZY? NUDGE?

I...I THINK I CAN FEEL WHICH BUTTONS THEY USED, BUT WE DON'T HAVE A KEY CARD. CAN YOU HELP ME HOTWIRE IT, GAZZY?

MAYBE...

JUST BE CAREFUL, GUYS.

YOU GETTING THE FEELING THAT THIS IS WHAT OUR POWERS WERE MEANT FOR?

KINDA WEIRD THAT WE HAD EXACTLY WHAT WE NEEDED TO GET THIS FAR...

KLK

AND BY OUR POWERS COMBINED...

...A GIANT CREEPY UNDERGROUND LAIR.

NO SKULL THRONE. MISSED OPPORTUNITY.

THIS PLACE...IT WAS A LABORATORY.

GASMAN? WHAT ARE YOU DOING?

TIME FOR AN OLD-FASHIONED '90S HACKING MONTAGE.

BACK ME UP, IGGY STARDUST.

HA... HAHA... ALL THIS TIME... LOOKING... FOR YOUR PARENTS...

LOOKING... FOR...FAMILY...

I TOLD YOU...I KNEW WHERE YOU CAME FROM...

THE SAME PLACE I DID. JEB IS MY FATHER...

AND HE'S ALSO YOURS.

MAXIMUM...?

WE FOUND THIS...

THEY'RE...

THEY'RE... ADDRESSES.

THE STORY CONTINUES IN...
MAX RIDE: ULTIMATE FLIGHT

MAX RIDE #1 COVER
by STEPHANIE HANS

MAX RIDE #1 ACTION FIGURE VARIANT COVER
by JOHN TYLER CHRISTOPHER

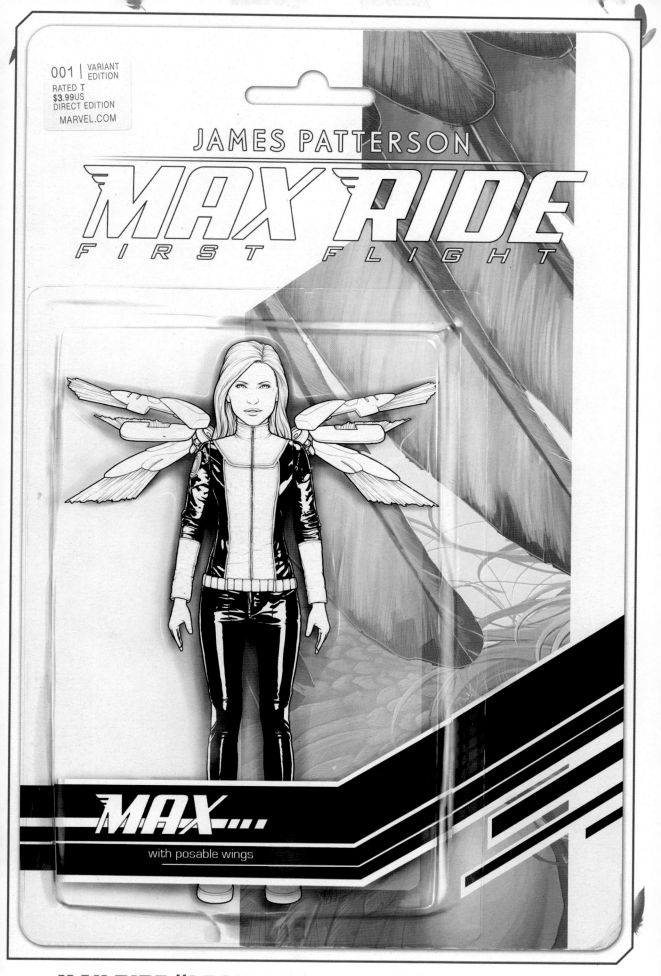

MAX RIDE #1 B&W ACTION FIGURE VARIANT COVER
by JOHN TYLER CHRISTOPHER

MAX RIDE #1 VARIANT COVER
by DUSTIN NGUYEN

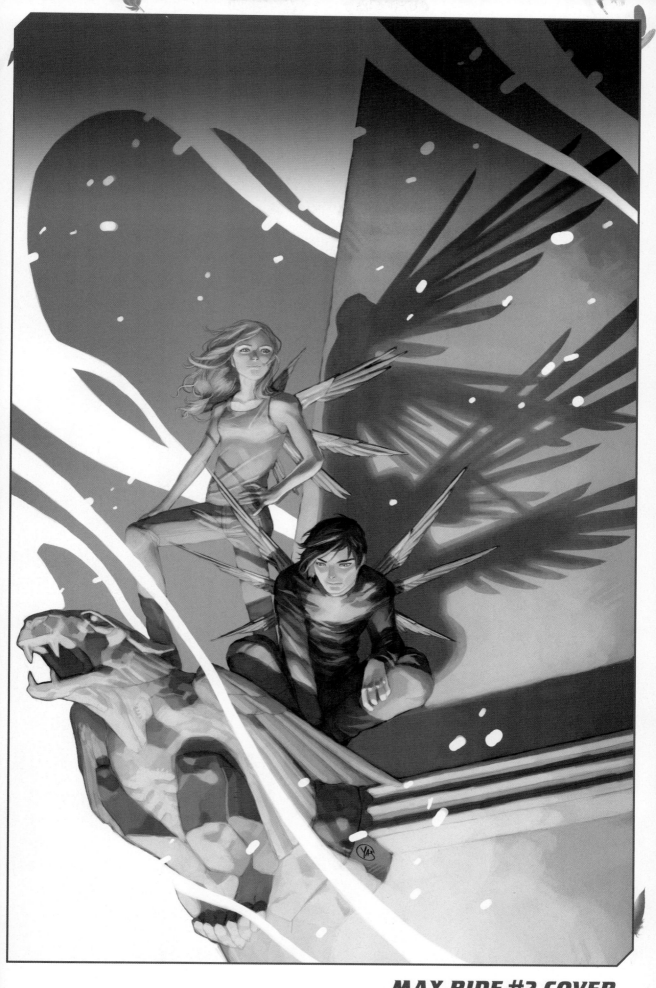

MAX RIDE #2 COVER
by YASMINE PUTRI

MAX RIDE #3 COVER
by STEPHANIE HANS

MAX RIDE #4 COVER
by STEPHANIE HANS

MAX RIDE #5 COVER
by STEPHANIE HANS

MAX RIDE

MAX EYES

MAX CHARACTER DESIGNS
by ALEX SANCHEZ

NUDGE

IGGY

ANGEL

-MAX

FANG-

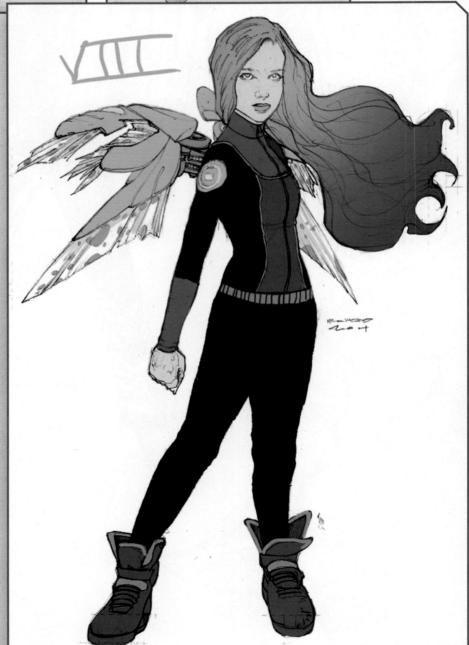

MAX WING MECH DESIGNS
by ALEX SANCHEZ

NUDGE CHARACTER DESIGN
by ALEX SANCHEZ

FANG CHARACTER DESIGNS
by ALEX SANCHEZ

IGGY & FANG CHARACTER DESIGNS
by ALEX SANCHEZ

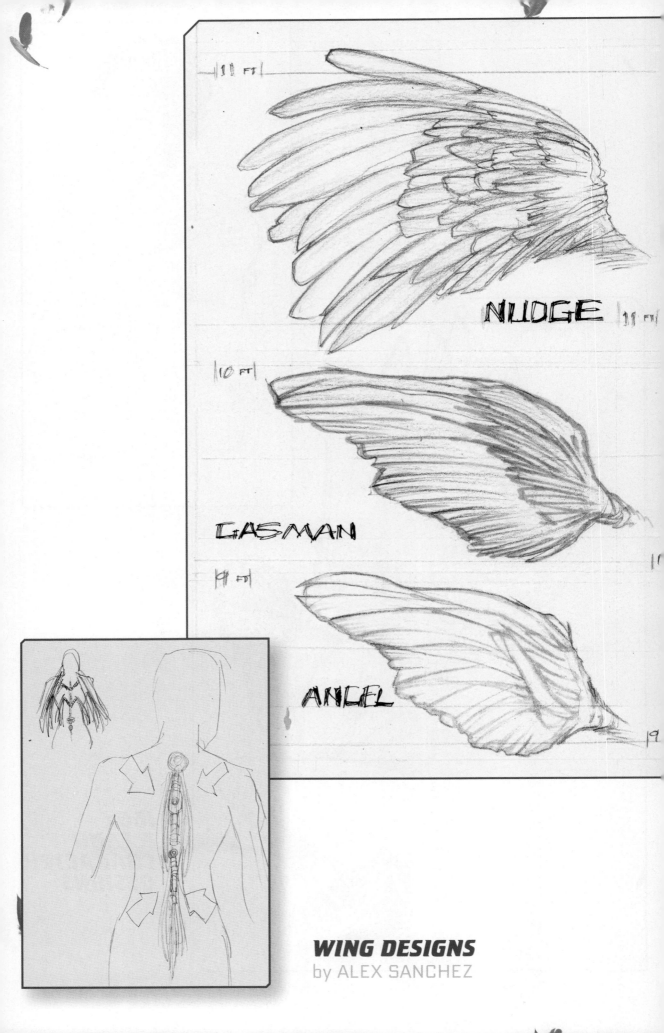

NUDGE

GASMAN

ANGEL

WING DESIGNS
by ALEX SANCHEZ

|13 FT|

MAX

|13 FT|
|12½ FT|

FANG

|12½ FT|

|14 FT|

IGGY

|14 FT|

ART PROCESS FROM LAYOUTS TO COLOR

Issue 1, page 1
by ALEX SANCHEZ
& ESTHER SANZ

Issue 1, pages 2-3
by ALEX SANCHEZ & ESTHER SANZ

Issue 1, page 8
by ALEX SANCHEZ
& ESTHER SANZ

Issue 3, page 19
by ALEX SANCHEZ,
MARK PENNINGTON,
& ESTHER SANZ

Issue 4, page 3
by ALEX SANCHEZ,
MARK PENNINGTON.
& ESTHER SANZ

Issue 5, page 10
by ALEX SANCHEZ,
MARK PENNINGTON,
& ESTHER SANZ

INSTRUCTIONS

GLIDER FOLDING INSTRUCTIONS

MAX RIDE WINGED GLIDER
promotional artwork by JOHN TYLER CHRISTOPHER